TIME DIMENSION BOY

Dev Ross

dizzyemupublishing.com

DIZZY EMU PUBLISHING

1714 N McCadden Place, Hollywood, Los Angeles 90028

dizzyemupublishing.com

Time Dimension Boy
Dev Ross

First published in the United States
in 2022 by Dizzy Emu Publishing

dizzyemupublishing.com

TIME DIMENSION BOY

Dev Ross

Time Dimension Boy

Written by

Dev Ross

LOGLINE: A smart-ass kid falls through a trashcan into a dimension
where he's the unlikely hero of a prophecy.

WGA: 2020

Dev Ross Productions LLC
928.301.4222
Devoross@gmail.com

FADE IN:

EXT. ANCIENT CHINESE FORTRESS - DUSK - THE PAST

The sinking sun ribbons the sky with red and orange, fiercely
illuminating the ancient fortress standing guard amidst
softly rolling hills.

PUSH IN ON FORTRESS wall.

A lone SOLDIER stands watch. XIAHOU, hard of body and proud,
scans the growing darkness for anything unusual. But even his
steadfast attention is drawn to the sweet melody of a
NIGHTINGALE.

His hard lined face softens as he observes the BIRD alighting
on the wall nearby.

                    XIAHOU
          It's early for your song,
          Nightingale. It's not yet dark.
          Perhaps you have come to help
          restore our Emperor's health.

BELOW - unseen by Xiahou, THREE stealthy shapes move quickly
along the exterior wall...

BACK TO XIAHOU - smiling, approaching the bird.

Meanwhile, the three intruders climb the wall.

XIAHOU hears them, turns to see the intruders breaching the
wall.

He draws his sword, expertly fights, sends the three flying
off the barrier wall. But as he looks down, he sees dozens
more charging forward while others swarm the wall like rats.

XIAHOU sounds the alarm - a huge GONG.

IN THE COURTYARD, lessor guards scurry to battle.

XIAHOU races to the wall's ledge, leaps down onto...

INT. COURTYARD - ON STAIRWAY - CONTINUOUS

... a stone stairway as two more intruders with drawn swords,
hurry up it. Xiahou charges them.

                    XIAHOU
          Aaaaa!

He forces his foes off the staircase and then bounds up the rest of the stairs to a small door. He throws it open and then hurries inside...

INT. CASTLE - CONTINUOUS

He moves quickly along a corridor to a tiny curtained alcove. He quickly checks to see if anyone is coming and then ducks behind the curtains...

INT. SECRET PASSAGEWAY - CONTINUOUS

Xiahou makes his way through the narrow torch lit passage. Someone is approaching!

                    ADVISOR ONE (O.S.)
               <Laughing derisively>

Xiahou slips into the shadows as...

TWO OF THE KING'S ADVISORS approach. One of them holds the Nightingale in a cage.

                    ADVISOR ONE
          The Emperor's most trusted guard,
          made the fool by his love of birds!
          Ha!

                    ADVISOR TWO
          Our cleverness shall be generously
          rewarded by our new leader!

Furious, Xiahou leaps out in front of them.

                    XIAHOU
          Traitors!

                    ADVISOR TWO
          I prefer calling us wise - as you
          would be to join us.

                    XIAHOU
          I would *never* betray our Emperor!

Xiahou raises his sword to strike...

                    XIAHOU (CONT'D)
               <Angry snarl!>

... but the two Advisors simply smile and then part to reveal several of the intruders coming up from behind them.

                    ADVISOR TWO
          He's been taking far too long to
          die, but he will be dead soon. Our
          assassins are already on their way.

XIAHOU reacts skillfully to dodge the dagger <WHIZZING> past
his head.

He turns and escapes with the intruders in hot pursuit.

XIAHOU ducks into another corridor, finds a notch on the
stone wall, presses it.

A stone door slides open. Xiahou enters and it closes just
seconds before the intruders hurry past.

INT. HIDDEN TUNNEL TO KING'S CHAMBERS

Xiahou springs up a steep staircase and then races down a
narrow corridor towards the King's chambers.

Ahead of him, assassins are already hacking away at the heavy
wooden door.

Xiahou charges toward them...

                    XIAHOU
          Aaaaaaaa!!!!

But suddenly, a glowing, swirling light forms behind him. A
stiff <WIND> kicks up and, helpless against it, a horrified
and bewildered Xiahou is sucked backwards into a vortex of
swirling light.

INT. VORTEX - CONTINUOUS

Xiahou falls backward through a funnel of light and color...

                    XIAHOU
          My Emperor!!!

                                        DISSOLVE TO:

EXT. HIGH TECH MEDICAL RESEARCH CENTER - FUTURE - DAY

An ultra modern building stands monolithic and gleaming
amidst pristine lawns and gardens. In front of the building a
towering statue glorifies the sinewy splendor of the human
body.

INT. MEDICAL CENTER - FUTURE - DAY

A TEAM OF SIX SURGICAL DOCTORS are in the final throes of an
operation.

                    DR. ZEE
          As you can see doctors, I've
          inflected extensive damage to Eve's
          synthetic brain.

ON EVE, the subject. Though scars and stitches cover her
synthesized skin, there is a strange softness and curious
attraction about her. Her glassy eyes stare.

Dr. Zee prepares to inject a serum into her bald head.

                    DR. ZEE (CONT'D)
          But with this injection of my
          experimental serum...

He sticks the needle in, causing the skin around the
injection sight to glow.

                    DR. ZEE
          ...we should see her recover all
          cerebral functions almost
          immediately.

Dr. Zee one of the other doctor's skeptical look...

                    DR. ZEE (CONT'D)
          In fact, her brain could end up
          being synaptically enhanced.

A <BEEPING> MONITOR shows Eve's already diminished brain
waves growing weaker until... flat line.

                    DR. ZEE (CONT'D)
          What?! This isn't possible. By all
          calculations this should have
          worked!

The skeptical doctor gives him a smug look and then exits
along with the other grumbling doctors.

                    DOCTORS
          <A waste of our time. And our
          research money. He should be
          fired...>

Dr. Zee hangs back to place his hand over Eve's, which has
obviously been sewn on and mismatches the color of her arm.

                    DR. ZEE
          I'm sorry, Eve.

WIDER to see that the Skeptical Doctor has been observing.

                    SKEPTICAL DOCTOR
          It's not as though she has
          feelings.

Dr. Zee's face softens.

                    DR. ZEE
          She could have.

WIDER as he motions to an Attendant.

                    DR. ZEE (CONT'D)
          Tag her for termination.

EVE stares blank-eyed as the attendant staples her ear with a
RED TERMINATION TAG.

INT. RECOVERY ROOM - DAY

Synthezoids like Eve tread in mindless circles or lay in beds
while recovering from medical procedures.

THE ATTENDANT rolls Eve into their midst and then exits.

EVE stares mindlessly when... a tiny glimmer of awareness
flickers in her eyes. The glimmer grows. Eve's eyes shut and
then open with a startling awareness.

Gasping, she sits up!

                    EVE
          <Gasp!>

Eve looks around to see other synthezoids, shuffling, or
staring mindlessly from their beds. Frightened, she slides
off her gurney and then moves unsteadily as she bump into
shambling synthezoids, as she makes her way to the door.

INT. MEDICAL CENTER - CORRIDOR - CONTINUOUS

She checks the corridor and quickly surmises there are too
many medical workers out there for her safe escape. In
response, she holds the door wider so to let the meandering
zoids file out into the corridor. Eve joins the ranks of the
mindless zoids as they shuffle along the corridor. Behind
her, ATTENDANT TWO reacts in alarm. He checks inside the
nearly empty room and then sounds the ALARM.

DR. ZEE pushes his way through the zoids to find the
Attendant.

                    DR. ZEE
          What's going on?! How did they get
          out?!

                    ATTENDANT TWO
          I don't know! Someone must have let
          them out from the inside!

                    DR. ZEE
          That's ridiculous! Brain dead zoids
          aren't capable of--
               (A thought strikes him)
          Unless...

The ramifications hit him.

                    DR. ZEE (CONT'D)
          Find her! Now!

Meanwhile...

EVE slips into an opening elevator.

INT. ELEVATOR - CLOSE ON EVE

Eve reacts in alarm as...

ANOTHER ATTENDANT pulls in a gurney stacked with TERMINATED
ZOIDS - all clearly marked with red tags.

The attendant glances at her but she turns her head away and
quickly pulls off her red tag.

The elevator descends a few floors, the door opens and the
ATTENDANT rolls the zoids out.

INT. ZOID RECYCLING ROOM

Eve hurries out of the elevator and then comes to a dead stop
as she reacts to the horror in front of her.

                    EVE
          <Gasp!>

She's in a room filled with stacks of synthetic body parts:
hands, legs, heads...

                    WORKER (O.S.)
          You! Zoid!

The worker carries a pile of zoid arms.

> WORKER (CONT'D)
> You don't belong in here!

EVE flees back into the elevator. The door closes.

EXT. ROOF - DAY

Eve hurries along the roof, stopping only a moment to gaze in wonder at the magnificent city below. She reacts to...

> ATTENDENT
> There she is!

Attendants head in pursuit with Dr. Zee following.

> DR. ZEE
> Eve, wait! Only one more procedure,
> I promise!

Eve runs from them. She climbs up to the roof's edge then turns from side to side not knowing where to go or what to do. She faces away from her pursuers and looks out over the incredible city that lies below. She closes her eyes and begins to fall toward it when...

...AN ERRIE LIGHT erupts in front of her and then sucks her inside its swirling vortex...

INT. VORTEX - CONTINUOUS

Like Xiahou before her, Eve falls through swirling strands of light and color toward the darkness below.

> DISSOLVE TO:

EXT. CITY STREET - THE PRESENT - DAY

An ADOLESCENT BOY and GIRL push KEE, a smaller, skinnier, grubbier boy around between them.

> BOY
> C'mon, fight back, you homeless
> thief!

> GIRL
> Loser!

Despite being pushed, Kee holds tight to a tattered pillow case that is stuffed with his stuff. The Boy grabs it away.

> KEE
> Give that back!

                    BOY
          Make me!

Kee runs full on into the bigger boy, tackling him.

                    KEE
          Aaaaaa!

The Girl dog piles on.

LOW ANGLE ON THEIR LEGS - As the other boys scuffle...

                    BOY
          Hey, you hit me!

                    GIRL
          Only because you hit me!

...Kee crawls out from between their tangle of legs. His
pillow bulging now with more stuff.

He gets a safe distance away and then turns back toward the
still scrabbling kids.

                    KEE
          Hey, guys! I may be a thief but
          you're the...

The bullies turn back to see Kee holding up his now more
stuffed with stuff pillow case.

                    KEE
          Losers!

THE BULLIES feel for their missing possessions.

                    BULLIES
          Why that-!/Huh?!

                    BOY
          My cell phone!

Feeling inside her jacket...

                    GIRL
          My pocketknife!

                    BOY
          Let's get him!

ENTRANCE OF ALLEYWAY - Kee tears around the corner PAST
CAMERA.

                         KEE
               <rapid breathing>

A BEAT, then the pursing bullies scoot around after him.

                         BULLIES
               <rapid breathing>

The bullies look around the dead-end alley way - lit only by
a single lamppost. There's no way out and not much place to
hide... other than a trash can.

                         GIRL
               Where is he?

Boy One strides to the trash can.

                         BOY
               Probably in here... with the rest
               of the trash.

He opens the lid and <SPITS> inside when, suddenly, a burst
of light emanates out, momentarily blinding him.

                         BOY (CONT'D)
               Ahh!

HE SLAMS the lid down, holds it.

                         BOY
               What was that?!

                         GIRL
               He probably found something cool
               abd I want it!

The Girl reaches for the lid when it <RATTLES> just a bit and
then harder and harder. The bullies fearfully back away as an
intense light BLASTS the lid straight up into the air.

                         BULLIES
               Aaaaaa!

As the light shoots up and swirls like a vortex, the
terrified boys tear out of there.

                         BULLIES
               Aaaaaa!

In a flash, the light is gone.

A beat then... WHAP! The lid falls back into place.

INT. VORTEX

Kee falls backwards through swirling strains of color and
light toward the darkness below...

                    KEE
          Aaaaaaa!!!!!

                              DISSOLVE TO:

INT. CAVE - BOTTOM OF SHAFT

                    KEE
          Aaaaaa!!!

Kee <SPLASHES> into an inky pool of water on the bottom of
the dimly lit shaft.

CLOSER - He surfaces, frantically swims for shore.

                    KEE (CONT'D)
          <Gasp! Excited, labored breathing>

He pulls himself into a seated position and then removes the
cellphone he swiped from a plastic bag. He switches on its
flashlight.

ON CAVE WALL - As the light searches the cave wall, it
illuminates strangely mismatched items that have been sucked
into a time warp of the past, present and future: a cave
man's club, a grandfather clock still <TICKING>, a futuristic
gizmo, a western wagon wheel...

                    KEE
          Where am I?

The beacon of this light passes over the fierce looking
Xiahou and then on to the front end of a car - WHAT??? The
light jerks back to Xiahou, who blocks his eyes against the
stark light.

KEE holds the penlight out in front of him threateningly.

                    KEE (CONT'D)
          Who are you?!

ON XIAHOU - standing tall and proud.

                    XIAHOU
          I am Xiahou!

Drawing his sword.

                    XIAHOU (CONT'D)
          Chief Guardian of his illustrious
          Majesty! Identify yourself!

Kee, still wielding the light, backs away.

                    KEE
          Whoa, relax. I'm Kee. Just a
          homeless street kid so... no big
          deal.

Xiahou blinks and again shields his eyes from direct light of
the light hitting him.

                    KEE (CONT'D)
          Look, you put that sword away and
          I'll put this...

He looks at the cellphone with its flashlight still on.

                    KEE
          ...this powerful LASER beam away so
          nobody gets hurt.

                    XIAHOU
          What is laser beam?

                    KEE
          It's a lethal weapon that cuts big
          guys like you into the size of me!

Xiahou readies his sword.

                    XIAHOU
          Demon! I'll not yield to you!

His sword slashing, Xiahou advances on a terrified Kee,
forcing the boy to step back and fall over some-THING.

                    KEE (CONT'D)
          Ya!

The THING <BARKS> frantically like a dog, only with a sharply
metallic sound.

XIAHOU raises his sword to strike.

                    XIAHOU
          Another demon!

                    EVE (O.S.)
          No! Please!

EVE rushes into view, shields the barking creature.

                    EVE (CONT'D)
          Don't hurt it!

CLOSER DOG - Eve quickly keys in a sequence into the Dog's
side, effectively quieting him.

DOG sits up <PANTS> with metal tongue hanging out, and wags
his metal tail.

XIAHOU, alarmed at the sight of Eve, raises his sword to
strike, but Kee jumps in front of Eve to protect her.

                    KEE
          No! Stop it! There's no such thing
          as demons! She's just a...

KEE turns his light to Eve, who attempts to hide her face.

                    KEE (CONT'D)
          Monster! Aaaa!

Kee races to Xiahou who stares at Eve with fear and wonder.

                    KEE
          Hey! C'mon! Why aren't you swinging
          your sword.

Eve blinks at them with doe-eyes.

                    EVE
          I will not harm you. I am Eve. A
          synthetic humanoid used in medical
          experiments for the betterment of
          mankind.

She indicates Dog, who sits up, front paws in the air.

                    KEE
          Right...
               (Indicating the dog-thing)
          And that... thing?

                    EVE (CONT'D)
          This is a Diatomic Obedible Gamate,
          otherwise known as a DOG. It's a
          robotic canine popular before
          hygienically appropriate synthetic
          canines were introduced. They were
          all supposed to be destroyed as a
          part of federation order LX98 --
          but I guess he escaped.

Eve stops and touches her head in wonder.

                    EVE (CONT'D)
          Like me. I escaped. This is odd.
          How do I know this? How do I know
          anything?

Kee looks back and forth between them...

                    KEE (CONT'D)
          Beats me. Oookay. So...let's
          figure this out. You and robo-
          mutt...

DOG <WHINES> disapprovingly.

                    KEE (CONT'D)
          Robo-DOG... are probably a part of
          some top secret experiment, but...
          since I'm not into conspiracy
          theories, let's just say you're
          from the future.

Eve is confused.

                    EVE
          The future? But it was the present
          for me.

                    KEE
          Right. Make that MY future.
               (Indicates Xiahou)
          And he's either from my past or
          from some Kung Fu movie.

At this, Xiahu grunts his disapproval.

                    KEE
          And as for me, I'm from the
          present, or my present. Geez, this
          is confusing. So, let's just jump
          to the end. What are we all doing
          here?

Again, Eve touches her head as she accesses new information
that lights up parts of her brain.

                    EVE
          We are here as a result of a
          coincidental anomaly brought on by
          a time-dimensional rift.

                    KEE
          Uh-huh.
               (Looks to Xiahou)
               (MORE)

                         KEE (CONT'D)
              I didn't understand a word of that,
              did you?

Xiahou looks extremely pained, guilty.

                         XIAHOU
              I believe... I am here as
              punishment.

He lowers his head.

                         XIAHOU (CONT'D)
              I failed in my duty to protect my
              Emperor.

Kee shrugs this off as he readjusts his stolen items.

                         KEE
              It's a cruel world out there. At
              least that's what my mom's loser
              boyfriend said when he caught me -
              but didn't stop me from running
              away. Every man...
                   (Regarding Eve)
              ...or girl-thing for themselves!

DOG's metal nose quivers and glows as he <SNIFFS>.

                         EVE
              Dog's nose sensors are detecting
              something.

His metal ears rotate. He crouches low, his tail up...

                         EVE
              He's engaging pursuit mode.

DOG takes off running.

Kee is indecisive for a moment and then, determined, takes
off after DOG.

                         EVE
              Kee! Where are you going?!

                         KEE
              After him! This is the closest I've
              ever been to having a pet and I'm
              not letting him runaway!

INT. CAVE - SMALL TUNNEL ENTRANCE - MOMENTS LATER

DOG rushes IN and then stops to <SNIFF> the area at the small
tunnel entrance before he sticks his head inside.

<SNIFFING> He <GROWLS> at something unseen and then bolts
into the tunnel. A moment later Kee rushes IN.

                    KEE
          Dog! Wait!

He hears Dog barking and so follows him into the tunnel.

                    KEE (CONT'D)
          I'm coming, Dog!

Concerned, he crawls inside...

INT. CAVERN - MOMENTS LATER

Kee steps out, awed.

                    KEE
          Whoaaa...

He's inside a huge cavern filled with crystallized
stalagmites and stalactites. His image is comically mirrored
in them, stretched and distorted.

                    KEE (CONT'D)
          Hel-lo....

He reacts to DOG's echoing <WHINING>.

                    KEE (CONT'D)
          Dog?

As his voice echoes around him...

                    KEE'S ECHO
          Dog? Dog? Dog?...

..Kee moves through the cave.

Meanwhile, DOG <SNIFFS> at something hidden in a rocky
outcropping.

One very round independent EYE followed by another, peeks up
over the rocks at him. Dog blinks once at them. They blink
once back. He blinks twice at them. They blink twice back.
The two eyes make room for a third LARGER golf ball sized EYE
to rise up between them. The larger Eye blinks at DOG, who
cocks his head in return.

THE BIG EYE rises up on a long stem as its iris rotates
hypnotically.

DOG regards the Eye curiously when...

Kee enters.

                    KEE
          There you are!

THE BIG EYE stops its hypnotic rotation.

KEE spots the three eyes now waving in front of him on their
long flexible stems.

                    KEE (CONT'D)
          Whoa!

The eyes blink at Kee.

                    KEE (CONT'D)
               (To Dog)
          If I can get you and even one of
          these eyeballs back home with me
          I'll make a fortune!

He reaches toward the big Eye, which darts back and forth
evading him.

                    KEE (CONT'D)
          Here eyeball... Nice eyeball...

Kee grabs it!

                    KEE (CONT'D)
          Gotcha!

He struggles to pull it free but it seems stuck. He yanks and
pulls, causing the long stem attached to the Eye stretching
out like a rubber band.

                    KEE (CONT'D)
               (stained exertion)

Then-- attached to the eyes is a huge half crab, half spider-
like creature that rises up from behind the rocks and <SNAPS>
its giant pinchers!

                    KEE
          Aaaaaa!!!

Kee, terrified, releases the big Eye which snaps back into
the creature with a <WHACK!>. It <SCREECHES> its fury as it
scuttles over the rocks after the escaping Kee. It chases Kee
and Dog chases it.

                    DOG
          <Metallic barking>

                         KEE (CONT'D)
          Help!!!!

DOG's metal ears lay back and his eyes turn red. His mouth
opens, his regular teeth raise up and long razor sharp teeth
drop into place as he pursues the creature.

KEE races through the cavern - his escape mirrored in the
crystallized stalagmites and stalactites.

                         KEE
          <Frantic, fearful panting>

Kee looks back over his shoulder...

THE CREATURE gains on him.

KEE turns his attention ahead when..

                         KEE (CONT'D)
          <Gasp!>

In front of him looms a solid crystallized wall. Mirrored in
it is the distorted shape of the creature getting closer,
larger. There is no escape! Kee turns and prepares for the
worst when he realizes the creature is futilely <SNAPPING>
its claws just inches from his face.

                         KEE
          Huh?

DOG's got the crab-creature by a leg and is holding it back.
<DOG SNARLS>

BACK TO KEE - Unable to reach him with its pinchers, the crab
sends its large Eye to do the job.

THE BIG EYE lowers itself eye to eye with Kee and rotates
hypnotically.

KEE's eyes mirror the rotation. In seconds he's mesmerized.

Stiffening, he falls forward into the creature's clutches.
With Kee as its prize, the creature shakes off DOG...

                         DOG
          <Yelp!>

DOG tumbles and slides across the cave floor toward the edge
of a cliff with a sharp drop off, and... it's coming up fast.

Dog's SHARP METAL CLAWS extend then dig into the cave floor
as the robot canine tries to slow his slide.

Meanwhile...

KEE is lifted upward over the creature's gaping mouth.

DOG slows himself to a precarious stop at the cliff's edge.
He just gets to his feet when the cliff edge crumbles away
beneath him. <DOPPLER DOG YELP>

KEE is about to become lunch when the creature <SHRIEKS>.

AN EYE atop the creature turns like a periscope and spots...

XIAHOU - his sword piercing the creature's foot.

THE CREATURE, enraged, drops Kee, turns to battle with
Xiahou.

KEE struggles to shake off his paralysis, stumbles, turning
his ankle...

                    KEE
          Uhhh...

                    EVE
          Kee!

EVE runs in and helps him move to safety.

ON XIAHOU AND CREATURE - Battling. <ANGRY CREATURE SHRIEKS>

XIAHOU takes aim for the middle Eye. With a slash of his
sword, he severs the middle Eye (leaving a long part of its
stem still attached) and it drops to the ground.

THE CREATURE, <SCREAMING> its outrage, scuttles back over the
rocks.

Eve tends Boa as XIAHOU steps in while sheathing his sword.

                    XIAHOU
          Is the boy injured?

Eve <RIPS> cloth from her own clothes and wraps Kee's ankle.

                    EVE
          His fibula indicates a slight
          exterior contusion.

Xiahou yanks Kee to his feet.

                    KEE
          Ow! My fibu-whatever! That hurt!

                         XIAHOU
               There could be more of those
               creatures. We must go!

Kee suddenly remembers.

                         KEE
               No wait! Where's DOG?! (calling
               out) Dog! Here boy!

Xiahou indicates the claw marks that trail over the cliff's
edge.

                         XIAHOU
               He died with honor.

Eve puts a hand on Kee's shoulder to comfort him.

                         EVE
               I am sorry, Kee.

Kee pushes her hand away.

                         KEE
               Yeah, well, if you think I care
               about some dumb-

ANGLE TO INCLUDE EDGE OF CLIFF - They react to <SFX: TWIRLING
PROPELLERS>. Then... DOG rises up INTO VIEW, his ears
twirling like propellers.

                         KEE (CONT'D)
               Dog!

XIAHOU looks, grunts, shakes his head, exits.

                         XIAHOU
               <Disgruntled grunt>

Eve smiles at Kee who is hugging Dog, and then heads off
after Xiahou.

Kee and Dog are about to follow when they spot something
inching passed them like a worm. It's the middle big Eye with
its stem still attached. Dog GROWLS at it, but Kee scoops it
up and, holding it away from himself to not look directly at
it, stuffs the Eye into his pillow case, the ends of which he
ties around his belt.

                         KEE
               So, Dog. How about we ditch those
               two and head off on our own?

DOG cocks his head at Kee questioningly and then heads off after the others. Kee SIGHS and follows after.

> KEE
>
> C'mon! We don't owe them anything!
> We didn't ask to be rescued!

> DISSOLVE TO:

INT. CAVE - FURTHER IN

The three, led by Xiahou, journey deep into the cave when strange symbols appear on the wall.

> KEE
>
> Whoa! Graffiti... Really weird
> graffiti!

THE SYMBOLS are clearly representative of chemical compounds and scientific factors.

> XIAHOU
>
> A secret code perhaps?

Eve fingers the symbols and then touches her forehead which brightens as more information flows into her emerging brain.

> EVE
>
> No, they're... they're symbols.
> Scientific symbols!

Her excitement grows as she points to the first set of horizontal columns.

> EVE (CONT'D)
>
> See! These are Hydrogen and Alkali
> metals!

She points to another grouping.

> EVE (CONT'D)
>
> And these are non-metals. And
> these... Monoatomic gases! But why
> would such symbols be here?

> KEE
>
> Only one way to find out.

Kee takes the lead as he heads off.

> KEE (CONT'D)
>
> C'mon.

XIAHOU reacts with displeasure. He strides ahead of Kee to
take the lead back.

                    XIAHOU
          I lead. Boy.

KEE reacts with displeasure but follows anyway.

                    KEE
               (To Dog)
          See what I mean, Dog? Grown-ups.
          Always gotta be in charge.

                                        DISSOLVE TO:

EXT. CAVERN EXIT - DAY

They emerge into the light of day... and a whole new world.

                    KEE
          From all that science stuff on the
          walls, I expected something more,
          you know...

REVERSE ANGLE - Before them lies a vast and barren realm
where a small sun shares the pink streaked sky with two small
moons. In the distance, a medieval castle fortress juts up
from jagged rocks.

                    KEE (O.S.)
          Modern?

                    EVE
          Perhaps we shouldn't go any
          further? I'm... I'm feeling
          fearful...

She curiously touches her stomach.

                    EVE
          Here.

                    XIAHOU
          Fear is the soul killer and is to
          be overcome always.

Xiahou leads them off again.

Kee follows, shaking his head.

                                        DISSOLVE TO:

EXT. CAMPSITE - NIGHT

It's a strange half darkness as the sun has only partially
set, leaving the two moons to share most of the sky. The
sound of night creatures dials up softly. A NIGHT BIRD
alights in a nearby tree and SINGS. Its song isn't like that
of a Nightingale but it's beautiful none-the-less.

XIAHOU roasts giant twisted ginger-like roots as the others
warm by the fire. He looks up at the bird wistfully and then
tears a piece of root off and hands it to Eve.

                      EVE
        Thank you. But it is not necessary
        for me to eat. I see you react
        warmly to that bird song.

                    XIAHOU
           (Reciting poem)
        Laden and weary is the winter tree.
        Yet in cold stillness floats the
        bird's song.

Xiahou offers the root to Kee. Kee takes the root and chews
on it very unenthusiastically.

THE EYE peers out of Kee's pillow case and scans his captors
before ducking back out of sight.

                                  WIPE TO:

EXT. CAMPSITE - EARLY MORNING

KEE softly snores when the sound of <HEAVY FOOTSTEPS> gets
progressively louder. <GROUND SHAKES> Still, he sleeps when
he's yanked to his feet by Xiahou.

                    KEE
        What? I didn't do it!

Xiahou pulls him to the higher ground just above their
campsite as Eve and Dog join them.

                  KEE (CONT'D)
        What's going on?!

Xiahou indicates o.s to...

A HUGE DRAGON approaches their campsite.

DOG <BARKS> ferociously until Kee snaps his metallic mouth
shut.

                         KEE
          Shhh!

                         XIAHOU
          Everyone down!

They duck and then observe the dragon as it tromps past
below.

KEE pulls out his pilfered cell phone camera, aims it at the
creature.

                         KEE
          Oh yeah, can't wait to post this...

POV through the camera lens as the camera snaps and FLASHES,
startling the Dragon. It looks up at our heroes then sends
out a ROARING plume of flames!

Crying out, Kee, Eve, Xiahou, and Dog dodge out of the way
just in time.

THE DRAGON spreads bat wings, springs up to attack.

Xiahou urges the others off and draws his sword.

                         XIAHOU
          Go!

DOG, <BARKING>, races out to draw the dragon's fire.

THE DRAGON shoots flames at DOG which he's impervious too.

Meanwhile...

EVE AND KEE take cover behind small boulders, watch as Xiahou
and Dog battle the creature. Dog leaps up on the Dragon and
sinks his metallic teeth into the raging creature. The Dragon
roars his fury, using his wing to knock Xiahou aside.

                         XIAHOU
          Uh!

Eve springs toward the injured Xiahou.

                         XIAHOU
          Xiahou!

                         KEE
          Eve! No!

As she does the dragon turns, <ROARS> at her.

KEE struggles with himself - should he or shouldn't he? - but then runs out in full view of the creature as it bares down on her.

                    KEE (CONT'D)
          Nah! Nah! Over here you overgrown
          cigarette lighter!

THE DRAGON turns its attention to Kee, who hops up and down wildly.

                    KEE
               (Ala Karate movies))
          Hi-ya! Ya! YA!

Kee's antics reflect in the beast's yellow eyes.

                    KEE (CONT'D)
          Ya! Ya!

The beast closes in on Kee, allowing Eve to get Xiahou a safe distance away.

THE DRAGON rears back, is about to let loose a volley of fire directly at...

KEE, who bends forward and hides his face when...

EYE, sticking up from the pillow case, stretches up on its long stem and directs its mesmerizing eye spin at the Dragon.

The Dragon beast is quickly mesmerized. Dazed, it falls flat on its face at Kee's feet.

ANGLE KEE, FEATURING EYE - As Kee stares in wonder at the fallen creature, Eye ducks back into hiding.

                    KEE
          Whoa...

Xiahou and Eve ENTER, Kee cops an attitude.

                    KEE (CONT'D)
          I guess you'll be thanking me now?

                    XIAHOU
          When your bravery is backed by
          humility, perhaps then.

Off of Kee's sour expression...

                                        DISSOLVE TO:

EXT. CASTLE - NEW REALM - DAY

In sharp contrast to the scientific symbols on the cave
walls, crudely carved shamanistic statues hover over our
heroes, glaring down at them as they walk the heavily rutted
path toward the castle.

DOG eyes the statues, <GROWLS>.

>   KEE
>   What are these things?

>   XIAHOU
>   Perhaps they are used in the same
>   way as in my kingdom.

>   KEE
>   And that would be to...?

ANGLE ON CASTLE - Two rough-looking GUARDS wearing furs and
crude armor, ride atop two crab/spider creatures like the one
they encountered in the cave.

>   XIAHOU
>   Ward off evil.

ON CREATURES - Each have a leather hood fastened over their
middle eye.

KEE registers this, pulls the Eye out of his pillow case.

EYE starts to swirl its iris at him but Kee clamps his hand
over it first.

ON CREATURES - Their other eyes swivel around and look in our
heroes' direction. One of the guards notices this and signals
the other guard. Both spur their mounts toward our heroes.

Seeing them coming, Xiahou places his hand on the hilt of his
sword. DOG <BARKS> in warning.

>   XIAHOU
>   Be ready to retreat.

Kee tosses his captive Eye up and down.

>   KEE
>   I'm not running from anybody, not
>   anymore...

Eve regards the Eye as he tosses it up and down like a coin.

>   EVE
>   Kee? Is that...?

Xiahou snatches the Eye out of the air and...

                    KEE
          Xiahou!

...looks at it!

                    KEE (CONT'D)
          No!

THE EYE swirls.

XIAHOU is instantly mesmerized and falls over. As Eve hurries
to attend him, Kee looks up as they become covered in
shadows.

                    KEE
          Huh-oh...

TWO GUARDS glare down at them from atop their creatures and
then pull the covers off the middle eyes.

THE EYES spin as the creatures extend their claws toward our
mesmerized heroes.

DOG <BARKS> annoying until his mouth is pinched shut by a
claw. <WHINE> He's lifted out of shot.

                              DISSOLVE TO:

EXT. OPEN AIR COURTYARD AND MARKETPLACE - DAY

Our heroes are transported through a medieval courtyard
filled with dirty peasants engaged in commerce.

                    PEASANT
          <Marketing walla>

Townsfolk stop to gawk at our heroes as they're carried past.

ON STONE ENTRANCE TO CASTLE - Our heroes are carried inside.

INT. ELDER MOTHER'S CHAMBERS

Flanked by guards, our heroes are left before a HOODED FIGURE
sitting hunched in a roughly hewn throne.

THE HOODED FIGURE lifts its hood to reveal a wizened woman of
unknown years. This is Elder Mother.

                    ELDER MOTHER
          So. You are spies sent by the
          Seekers?

XIAHOU puffs out his chest in indignation.

                    XIAHOU
          Spies?! Never!

Eve steps forward, bows.

                    EVE
          Please, we are just lost travelers.

Elder Mother looks them over very carefully and then turns
pointedly to Kee.

                    ELDER MOTHER
          Lost travelers? And you? Are you
          also lost?

                    KEE
          Depends. Have I lost my parents?
          Yeah. Have I lost my home? Yeah. Am
          I lost? No. I know right where I
          am. I'm here.

ELDER MOTHER regards him curiously then moves slowly from her
throne.

DOG <GROWLS> at her as she does but then quiets to a
<WHIMPER> as electrical impulses emanate from under her hood.

Elder Mother approaches the warrior Xiahou first.

                    ELDER MOTHER
          Give me your hand.

Xiahou bravely thrusts his hand out for the old crone to
take. <ELECTRICAL IMPULSES> emanate from under her hood and
her head snaps back into a trance.

HER EYES widen and in them unfolds a future where Xiahou
battles an unseen enemy. In a trance voice, she intones...

                    ELDER MOTHER
          When the two moons join the sun,
          two heroes will come to serve us.
          One, a great warrior.

She lifts her head back and regards Xiahou with clear eyes.

                    ELDER MOTHER (CONT'D)
          You are the warrior shown to me in
          visions. You are not lost but have
          been brought here to serve a great
          purpose.

Obviously moved by her words, Xiahou bows before her.

                    XIAHOU
          To serve *is* my purpose.

ELDER MOTHER to Eve.

                    ELDER MOTHER (CONT'D)
          And now your hand.

EVE self-consciously pulls her hands away.

                    ELDER MOTHER (CONT'D)
          Do not be ashamed. I know the evils
          done in the name of science.

Eve gives Elder Mother a hand. Once again <ELECTRICAL
IMPULSES> pulsate under her hood and her head snaps back.

ELDER MOTHER'S EYES widen then register an image where Eve
tends to the sick and injured.

                    ELDER MOTHER (CONT'D)
          You are the healer foretold to me.

Now Elder Mother moves to Kee. She looks at him skeptically.

                    ELDER MOTHER (CONT'D)
          Only you are not shown to me.

Her eyes narrow at him. <ELECTRICAL IMPULSES> jump around her
head as they register her upset.

                    KEE
          C'mon. No one can see the future.
          This is totally bogus.

                    EVE
          Her increased gamma wave brain
          activity does indicate an extremely
          high level of consciousness.

                    KEE
          Okay so she's all - Wooo... I know
          who you are! But what do we know
          about her?! Nothing!

The emanating electrical impulses coming from under the
crone's hood cease.

                    ELDER MOTHER
          I am called Elder Mother.

PUSH IN on her heavily lined face.

                    ELDER MOTHER (CONT'D)
              My people are The Servers...

Her eyes widen to show a visual history of her people.

                    ELDER MOTHER (CONT'D)
              Long ago they served masters called
              the Seekers...

HER EYES twirl until they show something substantially
different than the scenes before.

PUSH IN ON white jacketed SCIENTISTS huddled over microscopes
while entering copious amounts of data into notebooks.

                    ELDER MOTHER (CONT'D)
              The Seekers were a group of
              Scientists...

Then black suited MEN ENTER. They viciously knock over the
microscopes, smash computers, burn notebooks.

                    ELDER MOTHER (CONT'D)
              ...who left the small mindedness
              and the prejudices of their old
              world behind...

NEW IMAGE - The same group of Scientists, now with bags
packed, stand before a growing and opening vortex. PULL BACK
TO INCLUDE the slightly larger group of Servers, maids,
cooks, gardeners, trash collectors, and the like who will
accompany them.

                    ELDER MOTHER (CONT'D)
              ...for a new world where they could
              be free to seek out scientific
              truths and discoveries without
              interference.

The Scientists and Seekers pass through the vortex opening
which closes behind them.

                    ELDER MOTHER (CONT'D)
              But in the centuries that passed,
              the Seekers became increasingly
              obsessed with their work...

INT. SEEKER LABORATORY

A FEMALE SCIENTIST pours liquid into a beaker and watches the
reaction with intense concentration as a Server pulls in a
cart of food. The Server waits but then leaves as the
scientist never looks up from her work.

                    ELDER MOTHER (CONT'D)
          Their total absorption soon had
          them relying on the Servers for
          everything...

INT. SEEKER LABORATORY - LATER

Now several Scientists continue their work while Servers
literally spoon feed them.

                    ELDER MOTHER (CONT'D)
          Until the Servers became little
          more than the Seekers' slaves who
          did everything for their masters.

EXT. SEEKER FIELD OUTSIDE OF CITY

Servers toil in fields while electrical impulses emanate from
a highly modern building compound in the background.

                    ELDER MOTHER (CONT'D)
          The Servers toiled endlessly for
          the Seekers who sought nothing but
          scientific discovery and
          perfection...

PUSH IN on a bent over SERVER toiling in the field. He
straightens up, wipes the sweat from his brow, then glares at
the modern building of the Seekers.

                    ELDER MOTHER (CONT'D)
          And then finally, one day, the
          Servers had enough.

VARIOUS SHOTS as other disgruntled Servers also begin to
leave their posts.

                    ELDER MOTHER (CONT'D)
          So, they simply left and never
          returned.

BACK TO ELDER MOTHER as she returns her gaze to them.

                    ELDER MOTHER (CONT'D)
          We lived free for many years. But
          now we are under constant Seeker
          attack. I thought all was hopeless
          until...

She turns her gaze to Xiahou.

                    ELDER MOTHER (CONT'D)
          I saw you in a vision.
               (To Eve)
          And you.

She reaches out her hand to Kee.

                    ELDER MOTHER (CONT'D)
          You are the only unknown.

Kee takes her hand. Elder Mother's head snaps back. Her
irises fill with unclear images marred by haze and abstract
mists. Finally, she lowers her head to look at Kee.

                    ELDER MOTHER (CONT'D)
          Your future is not there for me to
          see.

Kee yanks pulls his hand away from her.

                    KEE
          Does that mean I'll be dead?

                    ELDER MOTHER (CONT'D)
          It means it's yet to be written.
          These are dangerous times. I cannot
          chance that you are not an enemy.
          Guards!

Xiahou, Kee and Eve are quickly surrounded by rough guards
with spears. They grab Kee and drag him away.

                    KEE
          Xiahou! Eve! Help me!

Xiahou moves to drawn his sword but Elder Mother raises her
hand to stay him.

                    ELDER MOTHER
          Your companion will not be harmed.

                              DISSOLVE TO:

INT. DUNGEON

A HUGE GUARD drags Kee towards his cell.

                    KEE
          Lemme go!

The guard throws him into the cell.

> KEE (CONT'D)
> C'mon! I'm just a kid! I couldn't
> hurt you Neanderthals if I tried!

The guard fumbles for the keys to lock him in when Kee
realizes he has an ace up his sleeve! He pulls out the Eye
and points it at the guard.

> KEE (CONT'D)
> Hey! Look!

The guard eyes Kee with disdain.

> KEE
> What the--?

Kee turns the Eye toward himself to see the Eye is sleeping!

> BOA
> Great. Asleep on the job.

THE GUARD locks the cell and with a smirk, hangs them back on
his belt before starting to leave.

> KEE (CONT'D)
> Wait! Comeback!

The Guard approaches and leans into cell bars with a snarl.

> GUARDS
> Yeah?

> KEE
> You got a bathroom.

The Guard smirks at Kee and then exits.

KEE stuffs the Eye away - this time into a pocket - and then
pulls the guard's KEYS into view.

> KEE (CONT'D)
> And I can always count on me.

He reaches through the cell and struggles to stick the key
into the lock. He's just about to do it when he's startled by
a familiar <BARK> and drops the keys.

> KEE
> Aa!

DOG wags his tail and <PANTS> eagerly as he enters.

> KEE
> DOG! Am I glad to see you!

DOG <SNIFFS> the keys and then, to Kee's horror, <CHOMPS>
them and <GULPS> them down!

                    KEE (CONT'D)
          Wait! What are you doing?! No! No!
          Bad dog! Bad robot dog!

DOG reacts with a sad face. <WHINE> But now he eagerly wags
his tail as he starts <GNAWING> on the metal bars.

Kee realizes what DOG is doing...

                    KEE
          Thatta boy! Good dog! Good robot
          dog!

In moments, DOG's chewed a hole through the bars and Kee
slips through...

INT. ELDER MOTHER'S CHAMBERS

She sits on her throne, head down as if sleeping when,
suddenly, <ELECTRICAL IMPULSES> surround her head. She sits
up alert and frightened.

                    ELDER MOTHER
          They're coming...

INT. HALLWAY - CONTINUOUS

TWO GUARDS escort Xiahou and Eve down a hallway when they
react to the sound of warning <GONGS>. Frightened, they
flee.

                    TWO GUARDS
          Uh!/Run!

Eve turns to Xiahou.

                    EVE
          What is it?!

The <GONGS> continue...

                    XIAHOU
          Find Kee!

Leaving Eve behind, he draws his sword and then hurries down
the hallway.

EVE, cringing under the continual ringing of the <GONG>, runs
off in the opposite direction.

EXT. CASTLE - DAY

In the distance, a swarm of flying Spider-like ROBOT DRONES
approach the castle...

EXT. CASTLE COURTYARD - CONTINUOUS

Servers run in panic as drones breech the walls and shoot out
synthetic spidery webs that engulf their prey.

                    SERVERS
          They're coming!/Run!

A DRONE nets a Server in its web, reels in his struggling
prey like a fish on a line.

                    SERVER
          Help! Help me!!

XIAHOU runs IN, slashes the Server free.

                    XIAHOU
          Aaaaaa!!!!

Xiahou turns to see several more drones capturing helpless
Servers. He frees as many as he can.

                    XIAHOU
          <Strains of exertion>

PAN AWAY from Xiahou to find KEE coming outside amidst all
the commotion.

                    SERVERS
          <Screams and cries for help!>

The <SOUND OF ATTACKING DRONES> permeates the air.

Kee looks upward. His eyes widen in fear.

A drone is headed right at him!

KEE runs...

THE DRONE gains on him then shoots a web out after him.

The web entraps Kee, causing him to stumbles into a heap
before is he dragged back toward the drone.

                    KEE
          Help! Help!!

Meanwhile...

XIAHOU no sooner cuts another server free when he spots the
ensnared Kee and runs to free him. But as the warrior fights
selflessly and furiously, another drone closes in on him,
shoots out its web and ensnares him too.

                    XIAHOU
            <Struggling exertions>

As Xiahou struggles to cut himself free...

KEE is being wrapped into a cocoon by his capturing drone.

XIAHOU free himself, fights back just as...

                    EVE (O.S.)
        Xiahou!

EVE hurries in.

                    EVE (CONT'D)
        Where is Kee?!

The warrior motions to where Kee is being cocooned.

                    XIAHOU
        He's been captured! Come!

The two hurry toward Kee when Eve is ensnared.

                    EVE
        Ah!

Xiahou hangs back to help but she urges him on.

                    EVE
        No! Save Kee!

But there is no time. Eve and Xiahou are engulfed in web
after web, after web...

Meanwhile...

EXT. ANOTHER PART OF THE COURTYARD - CONTINUOUS

DOG runs IN to find Xiahou's fallen sword. But he no sooner
scoops it up when he's covered in webs. He violently shakes
them loose when the sound of flying <DRONES> causes him to
look up.

Above, he sees the cocooned figures of our Kee, Eve, and
Xiahou being carried off by the flying drones.

DOG <BARKS> furiously and then, like any loyal dog, chases
after them.

He bounds toward the castle's protective walls then <PUNCHES>
through them like a tiny but none-the-less mighty
bulldozer...

                              DISSOLVE TO:

EXT. SEEKER CITY - DAY

The flying drones carry their cocooned prisoners toward an
ultra modern city - a gleaming city in stark contrast to the
primitiveness of the Servers' fortress.

Other than the stiff <WIND> whipping between the sleek,
windowless buildings, and the descending drones, nothing else
moves. All streets are devoid of life.

ON HUGE COMPOUND BUILDING - An IRIS opening lets the drones
in.

INT. COMPOUND BUILDING - CONTINUOUS

The drones shove the cocoons into empty shelves that line an
wall of the compound. In effect, it looks much like honey
cones created by bees in a hive.

ON ONE STRUGGLING COCOON as a hole is cut from the inside by
a pocketknife. Kee emerges, tears off the rest of the sticky
web.

                         KEE
              <Strains of exertion> Ugh!

He climbs down from his shelf then looks out to see...

Dozens of cocooned filled shelves. All cocoons lie deathly
still when Kee hears a moan...

                         XIAHOU (O.S.)
              <Moan...>

KEE heads toward the moaning cocoon when he hears a drone
approaching. He hides inside an empty shelf to let it pass.

Kee checks for other drones. The coast is clear. He makes a
run for it when the moaning cocoon starts thrashing wildly.

Kee turns back to help.

                         KEE
              Okay, okay. I'm coming.

He cuts the squirming Xiahou free with his stolen
pocketknife.

                    KEE (CONT'D)
          Hold still!

Xiahou throws off the remaining web, grabs Kee's knife.

                    KEE
          Hey!

                    XIAHOU
          Eve!

                    EVE (O.S.)
          I'm here!

Xiahou moves to another wiggling cocoon and quickly slashes
Eve free.

                    KEE
          I could've done that! Why do you
          always get to be the hero?

                    XIAHOU
          I am what I am... as you are.

                    KEE
          What's that supposed to mean?!

As Kee seethes, Eve pulls their attention to the rows of
other cocoons.

                    EVE
          Look! There are so many others! We
          must help them!

Xiahou starts toward them when Eve grabs his hand. She
extends her other hand to Xiahou, indicating the pocketknife.

Xiahou hands it to her and, with the precision of a surgeon,
she cuts a cocoon open. As the web falls away they see that
the WOMAN revealed is in a deep sleep.

Eve feels the woman's neck pulse.

                    XIAHOU
          Has she been enchanted?

                    EVE
          No... She's in stasis.

She indicates the rows upon rows of cocoons.

                    EVE
          As I'm sure all these bodies are.

Eve turns to Xiahou and Kee...

                    EVE (CONT'D)
          From their sheer numbers and
          condition, I must conclude that
          they're being saved for something.

                    KEE
          Yeah, like a spider saving a fly...
          to eat later.

Then... a GAS is emitted from a vent above them.

                    EVE
          It's a nerve gas! Get down!

The three duck down with Eve using her body to shield them as
the gas surrounds the cocoons.

                    EVE (CONT'D)
          That neuroleptic gas is what's
          keeping them paralyzed.

The gas stops and the air quickly clears.

                    XIAHOU
          Can we wake them?

                    EVE
          First we must cut them free and
          then expose them to fresh air.

                    KEE
          But that'll take forever! And what
          if we get caught in the process?
          I'm not being wrapped up again, no
          way! C'mon! Let's just go!

Kee starts backing away.

                    KEE
          At least we can save ourselves!

Xiahou looks back over his shoulder at him.

                    XIAHOU
          We are who we choose to be.

                    KEE
          Whatever.

He turns to head off when a drone alights in front of him.

                    KEE
              (Turning to the others)
          Run!

All three run but are soon surrounded by the encroaching
drones.

THE DRONES shoot out engulfing webs. Each of our heroes is
dragged toward a drone when...

KEE reacts to <BARKING>.

                    KEE
          DOG!

DOG races to the rescue. <GROWLING>, he grabs the web
containing Kee and tugs it backwards.

                    KEE
              Thatta boy! Pull!

Kee is the center of a tug o' war between the drone and DOG!
The robot dog and the drone yank him back and forth until the
drone's part of the web SNAPS and Kee and DOG tumble
backward.

                    KEE
              Aaaaaa!!!

                    DOG
          <Yelp!>

KEE rolls free but...

DOG is covered with web after shooting web and then is
dragged out of shot. <DOG YELP>

KEE scrambles to his feet.

                    KEE
          DOG!

But when a shooting web comes at him, he narrowly dodges away
and then makes his lone escape.

                    KEE (CONT'D)
          Uh!
              (Frightened breathing as
              he runs)

EXT. COMPOUND - STREETS OF MODERN CITY - DAY

Kee runs through the empty streets, his footsteps echoing.

He slows and finds himself amidst towering stainless steel
buildings with no windows.

The street is empty save for a lone <BEEPING> robot that
vacuums the street.

Kee wanders endlessly through the empty streets... Finally,
exhausted, he collapses to his knees. He throws his head back
to draw a deep breath when the image of a beautiful young
girl materializes on the side of a sleek stainless steel high
rise building behind him.

ON GIRL (NEURA)- Seeing him, she smiles.

                    NEURA
          Hello.

KEE reacts, turns back and forth while looking for the source
of the voice.

                    KEE
          Huh?! Someone there? Where are
          you?!

                    NEURA
          I'm up here.

Kee turns to see Neura's image on the building.

                    KEE
          Who are you?

An enchanting smile...

                    NEURA
          I'm Neura. Who are you?

                    KEE
          I'm Kee.

Another enchanting smile from Neura. Kee blushes.

                    KEE
          Um... What are you doing up there?
          I mean, projected on the side of a
          building.

Neura, flirtatious.

                    NEURA
          I was just about to ask you the
          same only...(giggle) What are you
          doing *down* there, standing in an
          empty street.

                    KEE
          I'm... I was escaping.

She seems very interested.

                    NEURA
          Escaping? From who?

                    KEE
          A bunch of whacked flying robots
          that shoot out these spidery, webby
          things.

                    NEURA
               (Alarmed)
          Really?!

Kee responds coolly.

                    KEE
          Yeah, well, it's really no big
          deal. I've gotten away from worse.

                    NEURA
          Oh! You must be very brave!

                    KEE
          Well... Yeah.

Then, he sees an image of a drone rise up from behind the
girl and begin to sneak up on her.

                    KEE (CONT'D)
          Look out! One of them is after you
          too! Run!!!

NEURA turns, screams, and then the entire image jaggedly
fades out.

                    NEURA
          <Scream!>

KEE runs away as well.

                    KEE
          <Frightened breathing>

But he stops himself.

                    KEE (CONT'D)
          Aw!

With that, he runs toward the building.

                    KEE
          Hang on, Neura! I'm coming!

As he approaches the building, an iris opening forms. He
hesitates a moment but then, determined, runs inside.

INT. NEURA'S BUILDING - CONTINUOUS

The inside is a sleek and empty as the outside. Kee looks
around when Neura's voice directs him to a winding staircase.

                  NEURA (O.S.)
            Kee! Help! Help me!

Kee, determined, tears up the staircase, climbing ever
upward...

Meanwhile...

EXT. MODERN CITY STREETS - DAY

A small cocoon hops its way through the street. It stops
then shakes itself faster and faster until, at a hyper speed,
it shakes away the cocoon wrapping to reveal DOG.

DOG <SNIFFS> out a trail then follows it along when he comes
across the small <BEEPING> VACUUMING ROBOT who sucks up dirt
and debris from the city streets.

Eager to make a friend, tail wagging DOG blocks the little
robot's passage at every turn. In frustration, the vacuum
robot tries to vacuum DOG up. When DOG won't be sucked up,
the vacuum robot sucks that much harder until DOG slides
partway into its mouth.

DOG wiggles and pulls back until he disengages himself. In
retaliation, he swallows the vacuum robot. With a <BURP> and
then a hiccup that causes his mouth to open and briefly act
as an air sucking <VACUUM>, DOG continues <SNIFFING> his way
toward the COCOON COMPOUND...

INT. COCOON COMPOUND

DOG <SNIFFS> around the corner into the cocoon compound.

HIS POV - the rows upon rows of cocoons lying in stasis.

<SNIFFING> DOG searches out a large cocoon - then - suction
cups protruding from his feet, he walks vertically up the
shelves to reach it. He drags it down the same way he came
up, then drags it outside.

EXT. COCOON COMPOUND - CONTINUOUS

Outside the compound, DOG VACUUMS the cocoon wrapping off to
reveal Xiahou, and then heads back into the compound.

XIAHOU breathes the fresh air and slowly comes back to
consciousness...

DOG drags another cocoon out of the compound...

INT. NEURA'S BUILDING

An image of Neura on a wall awaits Kee as he reaches the stop
of the stairway. But in this image she is crumbled on the
ground.

                    KEE
          Neura!

The image of her looks up.

                    NEURA
          Kee! The drone is gone. When it
          heard you coming, it ran away.

KEE reacts with surprise.

                    KEE
          Really?

He looks around uneasily.

                    KEE (CONT'D)
          But where are you... really?

Her mood changes and she's suddenly very grim.

                    NEURA (CONT'D)
          I'm afraid to tell you. If you see
          the real me you might run away.

                    KEE
          I won't. I promise.

She hesitates...

                    KEE (CONT'D)
          Look, I know what it's like to be
          different. People always picking on
          you, bullying you... But I'd never
          do that, least of all to you.

                    NEURA
          All right then... Turn around. I'm
          right behind you.

Kee turns around slowly, gasps in shock.

                    KEE
          <Gasp!>

ON NEURA - She is, in reality, only a version of what Kee saw
projected on the wall. In actuality, she is a frail, almost
translucent figure with blue-veined skin, slender appendages,
and an overly large head. Still, she is strangely beautiful
in an ethereal other worldly way.

                    NEURA
          You think I'm a monster, don't you?

Kee recovers.

                    KEE
          No...

                    NEURA
          You do! I knew it! I never should
          have shown you my real self!

                    KEE
          No! I... I was just surprised.
          You're really... very pretty.

Neura smiles shyly.

                    NEURA
          You're just saying that to make me
          feel better.

                    KEE
             (Sincerely)
          I'm not. Really! I know lots of
          girls... well, not lots. But if I
          did, they'd have nothing on you.

She smiles at him warmly. Awkward moment, then...

                    KEE (CONT'D)
          So... How did you get here?

                    NEURA
          It's been so long, I can barely
          remember.

She moves forward slowly and takes his hand.

                    NEURA (CONT'D)
          But now that you're here, I don't
          feel so lonely.

Kee, embarrassed, stutters a moment and then pulls her
towards the stairs.

                    KEE
          Um... Right. Okay. Well, let's get
          out of here! That drone might come
          back!

But Neura holds back.

                    NEURA
          Wait! Before we leave I've got to
          show you something!

                    KEE
          Now? But those drone things...

She searches his face with liquid eyes.

                    NEURA
          Please, it's important.

ANGLE DOWN LONG CORRIDOR - Neura leads Kee down the corridor,
his footsteps <ECHOING>, while she's almost floating.

                    NEURA (CONT'D)
          It's down here...

ANOTHER ANGLE - They reach an area that resembles the same
blank sleek walls as the rest of the building when...

                    KEE
          I don't see anything but a wall.

                    NEURA
          I'll show you.

Neura touches a spot on the wall. A section of the wall
becomes transparent and gel like. Neura moves halfway through
the opening and then extends her hand toward him.

                    NEURA (CONT'D)
          Come.

Wary, Kee takes her petite, blue-veined hand and follows...

INT. PROCEDURE ROOM - CONTINUOUS

Neura leads Kee into a sterile looking room with a large
circular table in the middle.

Forms of human bodies are embedded into the table in a circular pattern. Above the table is a frightening mechanical apparatus designed to perform an electrical transfer procedure.

                    NEURA
          See, Kee, once their testing is
          completed, the Seekers are going to
          use this machine to do something
          terrible.

Kee looks around nervously...

                    KEE
          I really think we should get out of
          here, Neura.

                    NEURA
          You mean, you don't care about
          what's going to happen? I thought
          you were a hero.

Kee is already backing away but Neura urgently pushes on.

                    NEURA (CONT'D)
          Kee, the Seekers are going to
          transfer themselves into the
          Server's bodies!

This is enough to stop his slow retreat.

                    KEE
          Wait. What? You mean the Servers
          don't have their own bodies?

Neura pauses...

                    NEURA
          Not anymore.

She reaches out a delicate veiny hand to pull him back into the room.

                    NEURA (CONT'D)
          You see, we've...

Catching herself, she lowers her head for a moment then lifts it.

                    NEURA (CONT'D)
          I mean, *they've* lost them.

Kee's eyes widen in disbelief.

                    KEE
          Lost their bodies? Isn't that...
          sorta impossible?

                    NEURA
          Nothing's impossible. I'll show
          you.

She moves to a blank wall and passes her hand over a small
section of it.

THE WALL becomes cloudy then disappears. And there -
suspended in another room in mid-air - is a GIANT BRAIN.

KEE falls back a few steps.

                    KEE
          <Gasp!> It's... a brain!

ON BRAIN - Feeding tubes with various colored liquids supply
nutrients directly to the brain, which is actually hundreds
of brains connected by thin electrically pulsing strands.

                    KEE
          I giant, humongous brain!

                    NEURA
          Actually, it's hundreds of brains
          all interfacing.

She turns to the horrified Kee.

                    NEURA (CONT'D)
          After a millennium of using only
          their minds, the Seekers' bodies,
          having become obsolete, slowly
          diminished into nothing.

ON COLLECTIVE BRAIN - Voices, involved in intense scientific
discussion, can be heard coming from it.

                    COLLECTIVE BRAIN
               (Various voices murmuring
               with words surfacing)
          "Ratio" - "kinetic" - "empirical" -
          "theoretical" - "experiment" -
          "speculative" - "analyze" -
          "equivalent"...

Neura regards the brains with disdain.

                    NEURA
          They had long ago solved problems
          like disease, aging, the
          environment - and so now all they
          do is theorize.

                    COLLECTIVE BRAIN
          "Hypothetical" - "conceptual" -
          "conjecture" - "classify"...

                    NEURA
          They talk and talk endlessly
          amongst themselves as if I didn't
          even exist!

Furious now, Neura turns and shouts at the Brain.

                    NEURA (CONT'D)
          But soon they'll be sorry!

                    KEE
          Neura, I don't understand. I
          thought you were a Server...

ON NEURA - the Brain pulsating and murmuring behind her...

                    COLLECTIVE BRAIN
          <Scientific murmurings>

                    NEURA
               (laughing))
          Me? A lowly Server? Never!

Her face fills with pride and anger.

                    NEURA (CONT'D)
          I'm a Seeker! But unlike them, I
          was born with this disgusting body!

She spreads her arms for emphasis.

                    NEURA (CONT'D)
          This... *torso* is a throwback to a
          time when the Seekers still had
          vestiges of bodies!

She turns and glares at the Brain with deep resentment.

                    NEURA (CONT'D)
          You should have done away with me -
          it would have been more merciful!

Regaining her composure, she turns back to Kee with an eerie
smile.

                    NEURA (CONT'D)
          But instead they kept me as an
          oddity, something to study. And
          then, once they realized that I was
          capable of fulfilling jobs the
          Servers once had, I was forced into
          a life of servitude.

KEE watches as the Brain continues to pulsate and discuss
amongst itself with no awareness of what is happening right
in front of it.

                    COLLECTIVE BRAIN
          <Various scientific murmurs>

                    KEE
          But why make you a slave when they
          have robots to care for them?

Neura approaches the Brain.

                    NEURA
          I'll show you.

She strokes it tenderly and it responds with a ripple effect
that courses through the many brains. The Brain responds
positively (humanly) for a brief moment...

                    COLLECTIVE BRAIN
          <Voices heard in a pleasant
          sigh...>

                    NEURA
          Because, unlike everything else in
          this world, the human touch cannot
          be replaced.

...but then returns to its ongoing scientific discussion.

                    COLLECTIVE BRAIN
          <Scientific murmurs>

NEURA closes her eyes. Electrical impulses begin to pulsate
around her head.

A drone drop down from the ceiling behind her.

KEE reacts in alarm.

                    KEE
          <Gasp!> Neura! Look out!

NEURA smiles.

                    NEURA
          Oh, Kee, you were so willing to
          help me because you were attracted
          to this...

She regards her body with disgust.

                    NEURA
          ...disgusting human flesh.

She orders the drone.

                    NEURA
          Take him!

THE DRONE moves toward Kee but he dives away in time to avoid
its shooting web.

                    KEE
          You're wrong!

THE DRONE shoots out another...

KEE dives behind the Brain...

                    KEE
          I liked your personality too!

The Drone moves around the Brain in pursuit but Kee stays one
step ahead of it.

                    KEE
          Now there's where I was wrong!

All the while the Brain is unaware of what is happening
around it.

                    COLLECTIVE BRAIN
          <Scientific murmurs>

The Drone closes in, shoots out another web. Kee ducks it
but in doing so shoves his body against a part of the Brain.
The Brain reacts with another very human sigh.

                    COLLECTIVE BRAIN
          <Pleasant sigh>

But this time it notices something different. Kee's touch
wasn't the familiar one of Neura's. Curious, the Brain sends
thin tendrils out and touch and feel Kee. There is no malice
in their searching out of him, only wonder.

                    COLLECTIVE BRAIN (CONT'D)
          <Questioning murmurs>

Kee has hesitated too long - allowing the Drone to rise up from behind him and grab him with metal claws.

> KEE
>
> Aaaaa!

He's tugged free from the Brain's tendrils...

> COLLECTIVE BRAIN
> <Disappointed sigh...>

...and dragged to the circular platform where he is shoved into one of the body imprints.

> KEE
>
> Please, Neura! Make it stop!

NEURA, meanwhile, satiates the Brain by stepping into the Brain's reaching tendrils. Sensing familiarity again, they withdraw back into the Brain.

> COLLECTIVE BRAIN (B-TRACK)
> <Scientific murmurs>

> NEURA
>
> I'm sorry. I know I'm using you but the ends always justify the means.

METAL CUFFS extend over Kee's hands and feet to secure him.

> KEE
>
> But I tried to free you!

Neura moves to his side.

> NEURA
>
> Silly, Kee. I don't want freedom. I want revenge.

Kee struggles.

> KEE
>
> But... But... You can't take my body! That's... That's *stealing*!

> NEURA
>
> And you've never stolen to survive?

> KEE
>
> That was different! I was hungry!

Neura flushes with anger.

                    NEURA
          You think your suffering is greater
          than mine?! You think I haven't
          suffered as their slave?!

NEURA points accusingly at the Brain.

                    NEURA (CONT'D)
          They need me but they have *never* in
          over five-hundred years asked me
          what I need!

Kee struggles against his bonds.

                    KEE
          Please! Let me go! I can help you!

Neura leans over him, smiles.

                    NEURA
          But you *are* helping me - by testing
          my machine. If it works I can begin
          the mind/body transfers. Pretty
          clever for a brain with a body,
          don't you think?

KEE realizes...

                    KEE
          This was never the Seekers doing.
          You're the one who ordered the body
          snatching all along!

Neura shrugs girlishly.

                    NEURA
          You think they'd stop postulating
          long enough to come up with
          anything so fiendishly clever?

Stroking his cheek.

                    NEURA (CONT'D)
          Now this won't hurt a bit.

She exits, and then...

                    NEURA (O.S.)
          Well, it might a little.

KEE's eyes widen in alarm.

EXT. COCOON COMPOUND

A handful of Servers recover from their stasis as Xiahou, Eve
and Dog continue to pull cocoons from the compound and into
the fresh air.

DOG drags out another when he reacts to an <ARC OF
ELECTRICITY> shooting up from Neura's building in the
background. He <GROWLS> and then - on the side of Neura's
building - he sees flashes of Kee struggling to free himself.
Dog <BARKS> excitedly. Xiahou and Eve look up and see Kee as
well.

                    EVE
          It's Kee! He's in trouble!

Xiahou turns to the recovering Servers.

                    XIAHOU
          We must go, so you must finish what
          we've started! Help each other!

He nods to his friends and off they go...

EXT. NEURA'S BUILDING

Xiahou, Eve, and Dog run inside and begin climbing the
winding staircase...

INT. PROCEDURE ROOM

KEE struggles against his bonds while...

                    KEE
          <Struggling exertion>

NEURA waves her hand over the wall which causes a console to
emerge. She enters a code into it.

KEE manages to slip one hand out of his binding cuffs. He
shoves his free hand into his pocket and pulls out the Eye.

                    KEE (CONT'D)
          Neura, please! You were right about
          me! I was attracted to your looks.
          I'm sorry! I couldn't help myself!
          It's just that you are so
          different, so special...

Neura, flattered, turns to him.

But just as she does, Kee pulls the Eye out of his pocket and
flashes it at her. But the Eye wiggles free of Kee's hand and
escapes.

                        KEE (CONT'D)
          No!!!

THE EYE CRAWLS away in the while Neura returns to her work.

                        NEURA
          Stop trying to distract me, Kee.
          Your chances of escape are
          precisely...

As Neura calculates, arcs of electricity shoot across her
head.

                        NEURA (CONT'D)
          Zero.

KEE struggles to free himself.

                        KEE
          But doing this can't be the only
          answer to your problem!

NEURA smiles.

                        NEURA
          I've done my calculations and... It
          is.

She's about to key in the last sequence when she reacts to
o.s. <BARKING>. She turns to face a <GROWLING> Dog.

                        NEURA
          <Fearful gasp>

                        KEE
          Dog!

<GROWLING>, Dog backs her away from the console as...

XIAHOU and EVE rush in.

                        EVE
          Kee! We're here!

They unstrap him.

                        KEE
          You came back for me...?

NEURA backs away from DOG.

                        NEURA
          Enjoy your reunion. It won't last
          long!

CLOSER - She closes her eyes and sends <ELECTRICAL> impulses
arcing into DOG's head.

DOG'S head <RATTLES> rapidly. His eyes register a change.
Now... He turns on our heroes! <GROWLS>

                    KEE
          Dog! No boy! We're not the bad guy!
          She is!

Still, DOG approaches... His regular teeth retract and
vicious ones lower into their place.

XIAHOU rips a thick strip of metal from the body platform and
raises it to smash DOG.

                    XIAHOU
          Stand back!

                    KEE
          No!

Xiahou hesitates when Kee brightens with an idea!

                    KEE (CONT'D)
          Wiggle it, Xiahou!

                    XIAHOU
          What?!

                    KEE
          Eve?! Weren't these robot dogs
          programmed to be just like other
          dogs?!

                    EVE
          Yes...

                    KEE
          Then trust me on this, Xiahou!
          Wiggle it!

Xiahou, feeling foolish, wiggles the bar over his head.

                    XIAHOU
          Like this?

                    KEE
          More!

Xiahou wiggles the bar more vigorously.

> KEE (CONT'D)
> See that boy! Wanna play?! Do
> ya?!

A change registers in Dog. After all, he is programmed to be a dog! <WHINE>

> KEE (CONT'D)
> Fetch the nice metal bar, boy! You
> know you want to! You know you do!

DOG wags his tail, <BARKS> eagerly for Xiahou to toss the "stick."

> KEE (CONT'D)
> Throw it!

Xiahou does.

DOG takes off after it!

> DOG
> <Happy dog wuffs>

Meanwhile...

NEURA makes her escape by backing up and then fading back through the translucent wall behind her...

> DISSOLVE TO:

EXT. SERVER FORTRESS

Establish then push inside to...

> ELDER MOTHER (O.S.)
> I was wrong.

INT. ELDER MOTHER'S CHAMBERS

Kee, Eve, Xiahou, and DOG stand before a deeply saddened Elder Mother.

> ELDER MOTHER (CONT'D)
> I believed my people were being
> kidnapped to slave for the Seekers
> as they once had. But to know now
> that it is not them responsible,
> but Neura...

She shakes her head in sorrow.

> EVE
> Do you know her?

Elder Mother pauses a moment and then...

                    ELDER MOTHER
          Yes.

Elder Mother lowers her hood to reveal her overly large head -
which is exactly like Neura's.

                    ELDER MOTHER (CONT'D)
          We are sisters.

Eve and Xiahou react with surprise, doubt.

                    ELDER MOTHER (CONT'D)
          Age is of no consequence for
          Seekers. We conquered it a long
          ago.

                    EVE
          But you allowed yourself to grow
          old. Why?

ELDER MOTHER stands slowly then moves to the open window that
looks out at the courtyard below.

                    ELDER MOTHER
          When I saw how my people's
          obsession with science was making
          them oblivious to human needs...

ANGLE OUT WINDOW - ON COURTYARD - The Servers below go about
their trading and selling business in the marketplace.

                    ELDER MOTHER (CONT'D)
          I wanted nothing to do with them or
          science ever again. I begged Neura
          to join me. Together we would help
          the Servers build a new society -
          one free from the evils of science!

                    EVE
          But science isn't evil. Its
          discoveries have helped mankind to
          survive and to survive better.

                    ELDER MOTHER
          Yes, better for some but not for
          others...

She turns to observe the people in the courtyard below.

                    ELDER MOTHER (CONT'D)
          In my sister's case, she chose
          science over people. She found the
          Servers ignorant and their bodies
          disgusting.

ELDER MOTHER stands with her back to our heroes as she looks
out the window.

                    ELDER MOTHER (CONT'D)
          Neura yearned to be like the other
          Seekers, to be accepted by them.
          But they were too absorbed with
          their work to notice her.

Kee grasps it...

                    KEE
          Which is why she was able to build
          that machine right under their
          noses.
               (Catching himself)
          Well, okay, technically they don't
          really have noses.

XIAHOU kneels before Elder Mother.

                    XIAHOU
          Elder Mother! I vow to you that I
          will stop her or forfeit my life in
          the trying!

She turns to him and smiles warmly.

                    ELDER MOTHER
          Yes. I know.

EVE steps forward as well.

                    EVE
          And I will do whatever I can to
          help as well.

                    ELDER MOTHER
          I know that too. It is why you are
          both here, as was prophesized.

KEE steps forward too.

                    KEE
          Yeah! Count me in too!

They all regard him skeptically.

                    KEE (CONT'D)
          I might not have been prophesied
          about but Neura tried to steal my
          body! This is personal!

                              DISSOLVE TO:

EXT. SERVER PRACTICE FIELD

Xiahou puts a group of Servers through their paces as they
practice with roughly hewn swords.

                    XIAHOU
          Engage! Ward! Bind! Cut!

KEE approaches Xiahou.

                    KEE
          Can I help?

                    XIAHOU
          No.

Disappointed, Kee leaves as the training continues.

                    XIAHOU
          Again! Engage! Ward! Bind! Cut!

EXT. SERVER COURTYARD

A small group of SERVERS look on as Eve demonstrates how to
wrap a head wound.

                    EVE
          Remember to make the dressing snug
          but still loose enough for the
          wound to breathe.

KEE enters.

                    KEE
          Anything I can do, Eve?

Eve smiles at him warmly but then turns her attention back to
her work.

                    EVE (B-TRACK, FADES OUT)
          No thank you, Kee.
               (To her students))
          Please remember to also check your
          patient's pulse and their eyes for
          signs of...

Disappointed, Kee watches for a moment, sighs, and then turns
away...

                              DISSOLVE TO:

EXT. SERVER CITY - CANYON EDGE - DAY

Kee, with Dog at his side, idly uses a makeshift slingshot to
shoot rocks into the canyon below.

DOG <WHINES> anxiously at something o.s.

Kee <SCRATCHES> behind DOG's ears when he reacts to the sound
of flying DRONES.

A SWARM OF FLYING DRONES head toward the Server City.

DOG tugs at him, trying to get Kee to move.

                    KEE
          They don't need my help so I'm not
          helping.

DOG <BARKS> at him incessantly and then, leaving Kee behind,
races off back toward the city.

KEE keeps slinging rocks then stops himself.

                    KEE
          Boy, me and my attitude
          sometimes...

As he shakes his head at himself...

INT. SERVER COURTYARD

Xiahou and his TRAINEES do battle against the drones. The
drones shoot out their nets, capturing groups of servers.
<BATTLE CRIES AND SOUNDS>

A TRAINEE drops his sword as he's captured.

                    TRAINEE
          Aaaa!

Xiahou comes to the rescue, fending off attacks as he
struggles to free the captured trainee.

Then, Xiahou's weapon is knocked from his hand by a shooting
net. All seems lost when...

KEE rushes IN like a screaming banshee.

                    KEE
          AAAAAAAA!!!!

He uses his slingshot to fire rocks into the flying web/nets
centers and sends them flying backward. This allows the
trainee and Xiahou to escape. Xiahou moves to fend off
another attack. Kee reloads his slingshot...

                                        WIPE TO:

INT. SERVER COURTYARD - LATER

The courtyard lies battle scarred. Torn webs, drone parts and
injured Servers are spread out everywhere.

EVE and her few trainees tend the wounds of injured Servers
as Kee, Xiahou, and Dog, all worse for the wear, approach.

                    XIAHOU
          You fought well today, Kee.

Kee is truly surprised at Xiahou's positive comment. A huge
smile breaks over his face when-

                    ELDER MOTHER (O.S.)
          But the battle was lost.

ELDER MOTHER slowly approaches.

                    ELDER MOTHER (CONT'D)
          And now... We are lost.

Xiahou bows quickly then...

                    XIAHOU
          Elder Mother, let us regroup and
          stage a raid!

                    ELDER MOTHER
          With whom? There are too few of us
          left. Neura has won.

KEE approaches angrily.

                    KEE
          No! She can't get away with this!
          We have to stop her!

                    ELDER MOTHER
          Only the Seekers can stop her now -
          but that is impossible for they
          have lost awareness of everything
          but their work.

Shaking her head.

                    ELDER MOTHER (CONT'D)
          There is no way to reach them.

The four stand in silence, contemplating their fates, when
Eve's brain lights up.

                    EVE
          Yes, there *is* a way.

Eve turns to Elder Mother.

                    EVE (CONT'D)
          I'll need a laboratory.

                    ELDER MOTHER
          No! Never! Science is not the way!

Eve cocks her head, smiles at her gently.

                    EVE
          But it is.

                    ELDER MOTHER
          You? -- who have suffered so
          greatly in the name of science? How
          can you say this to me?

Eve looks up at her with her pleading liquid eyes.

                    EVE
          Because it's true.

                                        DISSOLVE TO:

INT. DUNGEONS

Elder Mother leads Eve past the cells to a locked door. She
produces a key and opens the door to reveal an long unused
laboratory.

                    ELDER MOTHER
          I've kept it to remind myself of my
          people's past.

Then... <ELECTRICAL> currents light up around her head as she
senses the near future.

                    ELDER MOTHER (CONT'D)
          Come. We've little time before
          Neura begins the body transfers.

She leads Eve inside.

                                        DISSOLVE TO:

INT. LABORATORY - LATER

EVE mixes chemicals. Kee watches intently.

EYE peers out of a crack in the corner of the wall, startling
DOG. DOG eagerly pursues Eye, who ducks back into the crack.
Not to be undone, DOG <VACUUMS> Eye out of the crack and into
his mouth!

ELDER MOTHER AND XIAHOU - Elder Mother goes to a box on a
shelf, takes out a vial, and then taps out a tightly rolled
map from inside it. Using an eyedrop, she drops a bit of
water on the map, which swells to full size. The map shows a
series of tunnels running under the city.

                    ELDER MOTHER
               This map diagrams the secret
               tunnels running beneath the
               Seekers' City.

As the dampness from the water spreads, the map increasingly
shows more details.

                    ELDER MOTHER
               They were created in case the
               Seekers ever came under attack from
               the world they fled.

ON XIAHOU - pained with the memory of a secret tunnel in his
own world...

                                        DISSOLVE TO:

INT. SECRET PASSAGEWAY - XIAHOU'S FLASHBACK

Through a curtained haze, Xiahou remembers...

...himself hurriedly making his way through a narrow torch
lit passage. Then someone approaches! Xiahou quickly slips
into the shadows...

                    ADVISOR ONE (O.S.)
               <Laughing derisively>

TWO OF THE KING'S ADVISORS approach. One of them holds the
Nightingale in a cage.

                    ADVISOR ONE
               The Emperor's most trusted guard,
               made the fool by his love of birds!

                    ADVISOR TWO
          Our cleverness shall be generously
          rewarded by our new leader!

As the last of the above dialogue echoes cattily...

                              DISSOLVE BACK
                              TO:

INT. LAB - OUT OF XIAHOU'S FLASHBACK

Elder Mother regards Xiahou, who is still lost in thought.

                    ELDER MOTHER
          Xiahou? What is it you remember?

Xiahou snaps alert, then softens.

                    XIAHOU
          Betrayal.

                    ELDER MOTHER
          This memory pains you.

<ELECTRICITY ARCS> around her head as she reaches out to
touch Xiahou's head.

                    ELDER MOTHER (CONT'D)
          I will remove it.

                    XIAHOU
          No. I must keep it so that I am
          never vulnerable to such treachery
          again.

As Elder Mother nods knowingly...

                              DISSOLVE TO:

INT. LABORATORY - NIGHT

Kee sleeps slumped over the notes he's been taking while Eve
continues to work. She pauses a moment to stroke his errant
hair and then goes back to her work.

                              DISSOLVE TO:

INT. ELDER MOTHER'S CHAMBERS - MORNING

Eve, carrying a chemical compound, enters Elder Mother's
chambers along with a <YAWNING> Kee.

                    EVE
          It's done.

ANGLE TO INCLUDE ELDER MOTHER ON HER THRONE - Xiahou stands
at her side.

                    EVE (CONT'D)
          This compound must be injected
          directly into the Seekers'
          connecting neural pathways in order
          to initiate their dormant brain
          radii.

                    ELDER MOTHER
          This will work?

                    EVE
          It did. On me.

Elder Mother regards her carefully.

                    ELDER MOTHER
          Then let it be done. But take care.
          It must be accomplished during
          Neura's 24 hour regeneration cycle.

                    KEE
          When does that take place?

<ELECTRICITY ARCS> around Elder Mother's head.

                    ELDER MOTHER
          It's already begun.

                                        DISSOLVE TO:

EXT. SERVER FORTRESS - DUSK

Our heroes prepare to mount three of the three-eyed
crab/spider creatures as Dog, wagging his tail, looks on. The
creature's middle eyes still have hoods over them.

KEE watches Eve swing herself into the creature's saddle and
then tries himself.

He lifts his leg up but cannot quite reach the stirrup.

                    KEE
          <Strained exertions as he tries to
          mount>

He manages to get his foot into the stirrup but loses
balance...

                    KEE (CONT'D)
          Whoa! Whoa! Whoaaa!!!

...and falls with his foot still hooked in the stirrup. The
effect: He's now hanging upside down.

Dog happily runs to Kee and <BARKS> excitedly.

>   KEE (CONT'D)
>   No! Dog! Stop!

CLOSE ON DOG'S MOUTH - As he barks, Eye - whose been trapped
inside DOG's mouth - leaps to freedom! But Eye is scooped up
as it tries to hop past upside down Kee.

>   KEE (CONT'D)
>   Gotcha!

EYE squints angrily as its stuffed into Kee's pocket.

Xiahou helps Kee right himself and then hoists him into his
saddle.

>   KEE (CONT'D)
>   Thanks, but I could've handled it.

Xiahou pats Kee's mount.

>   XIAHOU
>   Of course. In time.

>   KEE
>   So how does this thing turn on?

The warrior gives the mount a hind end slap! Kee's mount
takes off running!

>   KEE (CONT'D)
>   Aaaaaa!!!

HOLD ON XIAHOU as a grim Elder Mother approaches.

>   ELDER MOTHER
>   My belief in you and the healer is
>   complete. It's the boy who worries
>   me.

Kee, still trying to gain control of his mount, rides back
and forth in the background.

>   KEE
>   Where's the OFF button?!

>   XIAHOU
>   He's young and needs time.

Kee still rides back and forth in the background, but now he's facing the wrong way.

                    KEE
          Aaaaaaa!!!

                    ELDER MOTHER
          Time is no longer on our side.

                              DISSOLVE TO:

EXT. TERRAIN ON THE WAY TO SEEKER CITY - NIGHT

Two small full moons illuminate our heroes as they ride their mounts across the barren terrain. Dog trots behind.

                              DISSOLVE TO:

EXT. SEEKER CITY - NIGHT

Under the light of the two moons the Seeker City shines.

                              DISSOLVE TO:

EXT. SERVER ENTRANCE TO CITY - NIGHT

The mounts are crouched like camels in the sand as our heroes head toward a sleek metallic wall that extends in both directions.

XIAHOU checks a map.

                    XIAHOU
          The old Server entrance should be
          here, but I do not see a door.

Kee approaches the wall.

                    KEE
          There's a door.

He passes his hand along the wall until an area becomes translucent. Kee leads them inside.

                    KEE (CONT'D)
          Trust me.

Kee is about to enter, but Xiahou holds him back and goes first. Eve follows but first turns to smile at the irritated Kee.

                    EVE
          I... I find that I am very fond of
          you, Kee. I feel it...
                    (MORE)

                    EVE (CONT'D)

          (Indicating her heart))
     In here.

She enters. Kee pauses a moment to take in Eve's words. He
enters behind her with Dog at his heels. The doorway in stays
gel-like momentarily before it hardens back to a blank wall.

INT. SEEKER CITY - UNDERGROUND TUNNELS - NIGHT

Xiahou leads them down a dim tunnel lit by the light of small
suspended globes.

                    XIAHOU
          According to the map, this tunnel
          will take us to the Brain Tower.

They walk a bit more when Eve stops, sensing something.

                    EVE
          Wait.

                    XIAHOU
          What is it, Eve?

                    EVE
          There's been a slight atmospheric
          change. I believe we're in an area
          of anomalous dimensional shifts.

                    KEE
          You mean like the ones that brought
          us here?

                    EVE
          Yes.

                    XIAHOU
          Then we stick together and we're
          careful.

As they continue on...

Kee follows when he's hit from behind by a small object.

                    KEE
          Ow!

The others don't notice what has happened and continue on. He
stops to see what it was.

Lying on the ground a few feet from him is a shiny object.

He picks it up. Its a 21st century digital version of a type
of Fitbit.

                    KEE (CONT'D)
          What the-?

                    EVE (O.S.)
          Kee?

Kee quickly pockets the watch as Eve appears.

                    EVE (CONT'D)
          Is everything all right?

                    KEE
          Yeah, sure. I, um... have a rock
          in my shoe.

Leaning on Dog, he starts to remove his shoe.

                    EVE
          I'll tell Xiahou to wait.

                    KEE
          No! The rejuvenation cycle,
          remember? We'll catch up with you.

                    EVE
          But the dimensional shifts...

He's hit from behind by another object.

                    KEE
          I'll hurry, I promise!

Eve smiles at him uneasily, and then heads off.

Kee watches her leave and then is hit by another object, and
then another and another.

Dog <GROWLS> softly but Kee shushes him.

                    KEE
          Shhh... Dog... It's okay.

Now Kee turns to see...

A car fob, a soda can, and a tennis shoe being spewed passed
him.

KEE looks up to see a growing VORTEX getting larger and
larger as it continues spewing out modern day objects.

As the VORTEX comes into full bloom Kee realizes...

                    KEE
          These objects, Dog, they're from my
          time. Our ticket home has
          anomalously arrived.

EYE peeks out of Kee's pocket to blink at it too...

EXT. UNDERGROUND TUNNEL - ON XIAHOU AND EVE

Eve, looking worried, still follows after Xiahou.

                    EVE
          Kee should have caught up with us
          by now.

Xiahou looks grim then heads back the way they came.

                    XIAHOU
          Then we must go back. Come.

They head back down the tunnel, turn a corner in time to see
the last of the vortex close up.

                    EVE
          Kee...

                    XIAHOU
          This is why Elder Mother saw no
          future for him. Because there was
          none.

                    EVE
          He wouldn't leave us. Not on
          purpose.

Xiahou just looks at her and then, grim-faced, turns away.
With a last pained look back, Eve follows after...

                                        DISSOLVE TO:

INT. UNDERGROUND TUNNEL - STEEP STAIRWAY

Xiahou and Eve follow the map to a steep stairway and begin
to climb...

                                        DISSOLVE TO:

EXT. NEURA'S SLEEPING CHAMBER

ON BLANK WALL - An iris opening allows Xiahou and Eve to pass
through.

                    XIAHOU
          The entrance to Neura's
          rejuvenation chamber should be
          somewhere here.

He feels along the opposite wall until an area begins to gel
translucent. They enter...

INT. NEURA'S SLEEPING CHAMBER - CONTINUOUS

Xiahou and Eve enter to find Neura asleep within a light that
surrounds her like an enclosure.

Eve takes a moment to observe Neura.

                    EVE
          Sheis beautiful.

                    XIAHOU
          Your beauty, Eve, is something far
          greater.

Eve flushes, hurries to change the subject.

                    EVE
          We must find the door into the
          Brain's chamber.

XIAHOU moves his hand along the wall. Finally, a doorway gels
translucent. Seen through the wall - the giant collective
BRAIN.

INT. BRAIN ROOM - CONTINUOUS

They enter through the gel-like doorway and then stop to gaze
at the Brain.

                    XIAHOU
          Never have I seen such a thing.

                    EVE
          There never has been anything like
          it. Not in my world or yours.

ON COLLECTIVE BRAIN - The tightly connected brains are so
busy discussing formulas and equations, they do not notice
the intruders.

                    BRAIN
          <Scientific murmurings: Formulas,
          Equation, Ratio, Conundrum, ,
          Hypothesis, Magnatism,
          Frequencies...">

Xiahou nods at Eve, who reveals the injection needle filled with the brain altering chemical compound.

INT. NEURA'S LIGHT SLEEPING CHAMBER - CONTINUOUS

Neura's eyes snap open! Her irises reflect Eve about to inject the Brain. Enraged, she clenches her eyes shut. <CRACKLING ELECTRICITY> surrounds her head...

INT. BRAIN ROOM - CONTINUOUS

Suddenly, a drone drops in front of Xiahou and Eve, blocking them from the Brain.

Xiahou draws his sword.

>   XIAHOU
>   Eve! Now!

Xiahou engages the drone, forces it back out of shot.

EVE presses forward, is about to inject the Brain but stops to touch it tenderly first...

>   EVE
>   Please don't worry. I won't harm
>   you.

The Brain senses her touch and eagerly surrounds her with its tendrils while exploring her.

>   BRAIN
>   <Curious murmurs about the nature
>   of what Eve is: A bio-synesthetic
>   life form/It's empathetic/Extensive
>   neural pathways/Synaptic expanse..>

Taken aback, Eve drops the injection needle.

>   EVE
>   <Soft gasp>

It rolls to a stop at Neura's feet. She scoops up and grins in sheer delight.

>   NEURA
>   A synthetic humanoid! What a
>   delightfully perverse body you'll
>   make for one of my people!

She clenches her eyes shut, <ELECTRICAL ARCS> spark around her head.

>   DISSOLVE TO:

INT. NEURA'S BODY TRANSFER ROOM

Xiahou and Eve are strapped into the body transfer platform.
Two drones stand guard. Beyond them, images of the Brain are
seen through the back gel-like wall. Above them, the laser
apparatus sparks with <ELECTRICITY>.

> EVE
> There's no need for this, Neura! If
> I inject the Brain, it'll be aware
> of you at last!

NEURA - standing near the body transfer CONTROLS - regards
the injection needle that she still holds.

> NEURA
> It's too late.
> (Giggle))
> Like the villains of old, I'm
> already too consumed with revenge.

She begins to key in a code when...

> ELDER MOTHER (O.S.)
> Neura!

ON ELDER MOTHER - approaching.

NEURA is shocked at her arrival.

> NEURA
> You!

Elder Mother removes her hood. Neura startles but quickly
collects herself.

> NEURA
> Of course, Gamma. Unfortunately,
> time has not treated you well. Come
> to bid your friends farewell?

ELDER MOTHER lowers her head and concentrates fully.
<ELECTRICITY> arcs around her head.

NEURA's head snaps back as the strong thought waves of Elder
Mother impact her.

> NEURA
> Your thoughts are still powerful...

Neura sends her own thought waves shooting back.

> NEURA
> But not as powerful as mine!

ELDER MOTHER is struck hard. Her wizened body flies across the room like a rag doll before it lands in a crumpled heap.

EVE is horrified.

> EVE
> Neura! Please! Have mercy!

NEURA smiles cruelly.

> NEURA
> Mercy?! Why should I?! *She*
> abandoned me! My own twin!

> EVE
> Twin?

> NEURA
> Yes, not only are we sisters, but
> we are identical twins!

Neura sends waves of lethal thought waves to strike Gamma (Elder Mother) again and again.

> NEURA (CONT'D)
> How old and weak you've become
> Gamma!

She towers over her fallen sister.

> NEURA (CONT'D)
> But I can put you back into strong
> flesh! Soon all Seekers will have
> bodies again and you and I will no
> longer be different!

Neura turns, begins to key in the sequence that will start the transfer process when...

KEE sneaks through the gel-like wall entrance with DOG. He reacts as...

THE LASER APPARATUS comes on line and shoots off small sparks of <ELECTRICITY>.

EVE and XIAHOU struggle against their bonds.

> EVE
> I will NOT be used for anyone's
> experiment! Not ever again!

NEURA moves to the end of the platform by Eve's feet. She still holds the injection.

                    NEURA
          But that's what you were made for.
          What you were you will always be.

KEE appears from behind Neura and nabs the injection right
out of her hand.

                    KEE
          In that case...

Neura spins around to face him.

                    NEURA
          <Gasp!>

                    KEE
          I'll always be a sneaky little
          thief.

Kee dives toward the gel-like wall that leads to the Brain
Room.

NEURA shots a bolt of <ELECTRICITY> at him but he and Dog are
already safely through.

INT. BRAIN ROOM - CONTINUOUS

Kee approaches the BRAIN.

                    BRAIN
          <Scientific murmurings:
          Stasis/Viscosity/Quantum
          mechanics/Observation...>

He's about to jab the Brain with the injection when...

                    NEURA (O.S.)
               (Chorus of Neura voices))
          Don't Kee.

Kee spins to face Neura - whose image appears on many of the
stainless surfaces in the room. Her eyes are tearing up.

                    NEURA (CONT'D)
               (Chorus of Neura voices))
          Please.

                    KEE
          Why should I do anything you ask?
          You tried to hurt me and now you're
          hurting my friends!

As Kee turns to face the many images, the real Neura edges up
from behind him.

                         NEURA
                (Chorus of Neura voices)
           Your friends? People like us don't
           have friends...

He spins around to face the real Neura.

                         NEURA (CONT'D)
           We're outcasts...

She moves in closer, her big eyes imploring her.

                         NEURA (CONT'D)
           No one has ever cared for us.

                         KEE
           Eve... Xiahou... They care for me.

                         NEURA
           No. They pity you.

More of her tears gather...

                         NEURA (CONT'D)
           I was wrong to hurt you, Kee, but
           now I know... Now, I see it! We're
           alike. We belong together.

Kee lowers his head, nods...

                         KEE
           Yes...

PAN DOWN TO HIS HAND as he slips the injection into his
pocket.

                         KEE (CONT'D)
           You're right.

NEURA smiles.

                         NEURA
           Of course I am. Now give me what's
           in your pocket.

                         KEE
           Are you sure?

                         NEURA
           Yes! *Give it to me!*

KEE reaches into his pocket.

                         KEE
              Okay... CATCH!

He tosses it to her!

NEURA catches it, brings it up to her face to look at it
squarely. But it isn't the compound as she expected - it's
the Eye!

                         NEURA
              No!

The Eye twirls, mesmerizing Neura. Kee grabs the Eye and
Neura as she topples over. He lowers her to the floor, re-
pockets the Eye, and then hurries toward the Brain. But--
He's thrown back as Neura's invention kicks into gear!

<SFX: MACHINE REVVING UP>

                         VOICE OF MACHINE
              Transmission mode ready. Begin
              transfer.

<ELECTRICITY> arcs back and forth between Xiahou and Eve and
the Brain!

KEE watches in horror as...

TWO of the attached brains begin to pull away from the rest.

KEE raises the injection needle up then - bracing himself
against the repeated shocks of <ELECTRICITY> spasming through
him - inserts the needle into a portion of the neural network
that connects the many brains.

Kee is covered by the current. His body shakes horribly when
a huge <BLAST> sends him flying.

                         KEE
              Aaaaa!

ON BRAIN - as the <ELECTRICAL> currents still course around
and through it.

KEE recovers in time to watch...

THE BRAIN expand and shrink again and again and then, one by
one, each singular brain begins to light up and respond.
Finally, a continuous <ELECTRICAL> impulse courses around and
around the brain, moving faster and faster until the chorus
of Brain voices begin to separate.

                    BRAIN
          <Chorus of voices: What's
          happening?/Who is out there?/Where
          are we?>

CLOSER ON TWO BRAINS that have been pulling away.

                    BRAIN ONE (FEMININE VOICE)
          Neura, dear? What have you done?

                    BRAIN TWO (MASCULINE VOICE)
          Our collective now senses ill-
          intent.

THE BRAIN shoots out a bolt of electricity that blasts
through the gel-like wall and hits the laser apparatus above
Xiahou and Eve.

ON LASER APPARATUS - shorting, spewing electrical sparks.

BACK TO BRAIN - Now all of the brains have pulled away. The
effect looks like a swarm as they speak amongst themselves.

                    BRAIN
          <Collective urgent murmurings>

They suddenly become silent, then shoot out an <ELECTRICAL>
bolt that obliterates the wall and connects them with Neura.

THE BRAINS shoot out another bolt that connects with Gamma.

As the connection between the Brains, Neura and Gamma
continues, Kee hurries to free Eve and Xiahou. Xiahou grabs
Kee's arm.

                    XIAHOU
          Thank you.

Kee smiles gratefully then turns to regard the Brains - who
continue their connection to Neura and Gamma.

                    KEE
          What are they're doing?

                    EVE
          Talking to the sisters -- and
          listening -- at long last.

                                        WIPE TO:

EXT. COCOON COMPOUND - DAY

Drones still remove cocooned Servers from the compound and
cut them free to awaken in the fresh air.

Xiahou, Eve, Kee, Gamma and Neura watch.

Gamma turns to Neura.

                    GAMMA/ELDER MOTHER
          Neura, I would like us to be
          sisters again.

Neura turns away but Gamma persists.

                    GAMMA/ELDER MOTHER (CONT'D)
          I was wrong to cut my people off
          from science. Our societies can
          mutually benefit from one another.
          We can build something new...
          together.

                    NEURA
          I will never join you, Gamma.

NEURA clenches her eyes tight and sends out a mental summons.
In seconds a drone approaches and gently picks her up.

                    NEURA (CONT'D)
          Never.

With that, the drone carries her off as the others watch.

                    EVE
          I don't understand. Why would she
          choose such a path?

                    GAMMA/ELDER MOTHER
          Some fear change, even if the
          change is good.

ON NEURA - proud and stubborn as she's carried back into her
tower.

                                        WIPE TO:

INT. SERVER FORTRESS - DAY

Flying drones bring in supplies while other drones work side
by side with Servers to build a new and improved Server city.

PAN TO GATES OF CITY AND PUSH THROUGH TO:

EXT. SERVER FORTRESS - OUTSIDE OF GATE

Kee and Dog stand with Xiahou, Eve, and Gamma. A mount stands
ready.

                    EVE
          I wish you'd reconsider, Kee. We
          need you here.

Kee smiles and shakes his head.

                    KEE
          Nah. You and Xiahou are what these
          people need, not me. I'm just a
          common thief.

Eve gently touches his face.

                    EVE
          There is nothing common about you,
          Kee.

Kee smiles at her, turns to Xiahou.

                    KEE
          So... I guess this is it.

Xiahou eyes him carefully and then bows to him. Moved by
Xiahou's respectful gesture, Kee throws his arms around the
surprised warrior in a big hug.

GAMMA steps forward to bid Kee goodbye.

                    GAMMA/ELDER MOTHER
          My vision showed me two heroes but
          it was wrong. Here stand *three*
          heroes.

Kee grins.

WIDE - This time Kee expertly mounts the creature and rides
off. Dog trots after him.

                    KEE
          Well... Goodbye everyone! Good-
          luck!

EVE, GAMMA AND XIAHOU watch him ride off. Eve feels the
wetness running down her face.

                    EVE
          What is this?

                    GAMMA/ELDER MOTHER
          They are tears.

                    EVE
          I'm crying?

Gamma shakes her head yes.

Eve shows Gamma and Xiahou her wet hands.

                    EVE (CONT'D)
          I'm crying! See! Tears! Just like a
          human!

Gamma takes Eve's hands in hers.

                    GAMMA/ELDER MOTHER
          Yes, Eve, just like a human.

Together, they all look in Kee's departing direction.

                    EVE
          Do you think he'll ever come back?

                    GAMMA/ELDER MOTHER
          Of that, my dears, I am certain...

WE FALL INTO HER EYES which show us...

INT. VORTEX

Kee and Dog fall through the swirling strains of a vortex.

                    KEE
          (Doppler SFX) Aaaaaaaaa!!!!

EXT. MEADOW - NEW REALM - DAY

We're back in the world that Kee left from at the start of
the story. (Or are we???)

                    KEE (PARTIAL O.S.)
          (Reverse Doppler SFX) Aaaaaa!!!!

Kee and DOG appear falling from the sky, and then plummet
into soft green grass.

                    KEE (CONT'D)
          Ugh!

They recover and then look around.

                    KEE (CONT'D)
          Hey! We're back! We're really back!

Then... A huge shadow falls over them.

                    KEE (CONT'D)
          Huh-oh...

PULL BACK to reveal HUGE LEGS the size of giant tree trunks.

                    KEE
          Okay, so maybe we're not *exactly*
          back...

Dog <GROWLS>...

PULL BACK TO REVEAL TWO GIANTS - confused and scratching
their heads - as they watch a terrified Kee and Dog run right
between their giant legs and then head for the hills...

                    DOG
          <Fearful yelps!>

                    KEE (CONT'D)
          Aaaaaa!!!!

                              IRIS OUT:

                    THE END